# TITLE II-A

# KING TREE

## FIONA FRENCH

HENRY Z. WALCK, INC.
New York

A young orange-tree once grew in a garden where the sun shone. His neighbours, four handsome trees, quarrelled every day about who should be the king of the trees. Tired of all the noise, the orange-tree said:
"Let the ladies decide who shall be king."

The proud trees were so eager to please the ladies that they began at once to boast of how fine they were. The oak-tree spoke first in a deep voice.

"I am the oldest, and the strongest. I give shelter to small animals and birds. I shall live for a long time."

"Beware," said the laurel-tree in a sharp, high voice. "Old trees can be hollow inside.

"Follow me, and I
will lead you to

honour and glory,
splendour and fame."

"When I am king," said the pomegranate-tree, lazily, "it will always be summer. The garden will be green all the year."

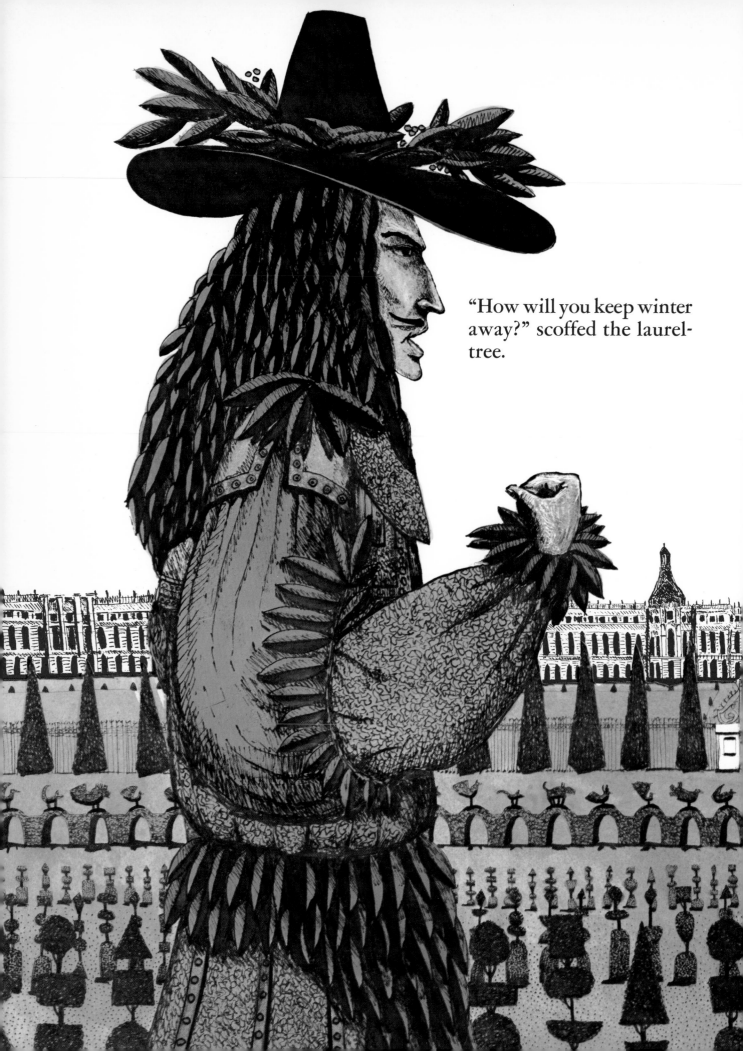

"How will you keep winter away?" scoffed the laurel-tree.

"You are just a tyrant, a bully," cried the pomegranate.

"Sissy!"

"Savage!"

"Oh, please, do not fight," said the olive-tree, in his gentle voice. "Your anger disturbs the whole garden."

"If I am king, the gar-
den will always be
calm. Storms may howl

at the gates, but inside will be sunshine and peace."

"Peace, who wants peace?" a vine-tree interrupted suddenly. "I don't want peace."

"I want music and dancing and bright lights; fountains of wine, and fruit from eastern lands; palaces of gold and ivory; pearls and diamonds, rubies and emeralds. I want flowers in winter, and ice in summer; festivals and carnivals, and rejoicing every day."

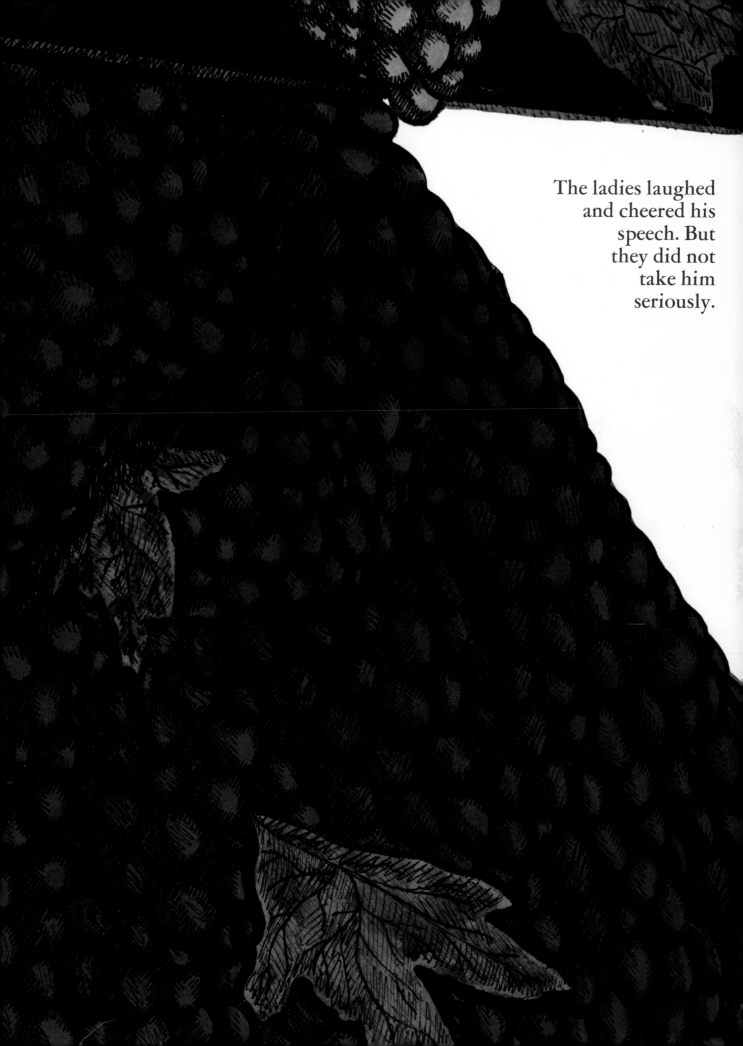

The ladies laughed
and cheered his
speech. But
they did not
take him
seriously.

"He cannot even stand up on his own," they whispered. "See how he clings to the wall."

Then

the
orange-
tree said,

"Now, ladies, you
must choose the king."

"I like the oak-tree, but he thinks too much of himself."

"The laurel-tree is clever and brave, but he is too hasty."

"The pomegranate has a heart of gold, but he is lazy and foolish."

"The olive is noble and good, but he lives in a dream."

"The vine wants everything, and gives nothing."

"I think the orange-tree is better than any of them."

"But of course," cried all the ladies at once. "The orange-tree is best. His fruit is like the sun, his leaves give us shelter, his flowers shed fragrance over the garden. We will choose the orange-tree."

So the orange-tree became king. "Thank you very much," he said. "It is a great honour. I will try to be a good king, and you will always be welcome in my garden."